# NANCY DREW®

girl detective

PAPERCUTZ™

# NANCY DREW GRAPHIC NOVELS AVAILABLE FROM PAPERCUTZ

#1 "The Demon of River Heights"

#2 "Writ In Stone"

#3 "The Haunted Dollhouse"

#4 "The Girl Who Wasn't There"

#5 "The Fake Heir"

#6 "Mr. Cheeters Is Missing"

#7 "The Charmed Bracelet"

#8 "Global Warning"

#9 "Ghost In The Machinery"

#10 "The Disoriented Express"

#11 "Monkey Wrench Blues"

#12 "Dress Reversal"

#13 "Doggone Town"

#14 "Sleight of Dan"

#15 "Tiger Counter"

#16 "What Goes Up..."

#17 "Night of the Living Chatchke"

Coming August '09
#18 "City Under the Basement"

$7.95 each in paperback, $12.95 each in hardcover. Please add $4.00 for postage and handling for the first book, add $1.00 for each additional book. Please make check payable to NBM Publishing. Send to:

**Papercutz, 40 Exchange Place, Suite 1308 New York, NY 10005, 1-800-886-1223**

**www.papercutz.com**

# NANCY DREW girl detective®

#17

## *Night of the Living Chatchke*

STEFAN PETRUCHA & SARAH KINNEY • Writers
SHO MURASE • Artist
with 3D CG elements and color by CARLOS JOSE GUZMAN
Based on the series by
CAROLYN KEENE

New York

Night of the Living Chatchke
STEFAN PETRUCHA & SARAH KINNEY – Writers
SHO MURASE – Artist
with 3D CG elements and color by CARLOS JOSE GUZMAN
BRYAN SENKA – Letterer
MIKHAELA REID and MASHEKA WOOD – Production
MICHAEL PETRANEK - Editorial Assistant
JIM SALICRUP
Editor-in-Chief

ISBN 10: 1-59707-143-9 paperback edition
ISBN 13: 978-1-59707-143-7 paperback edition
ISBN 10: 1-59707-144-7 hardcover edition
ISBN 13: 978-1-59707-144-4 hardcover edition



Printed in China.
February 2009 by WKT Co. LTD.
3/F Phase I Leader Industrial Centre
188 Texaco Road, Tsuen Wan, N.T.
Hong Kong

Distributed by Macmillan.

10 9 8 7 6 5 4 3 2 1

NANCY DREW, GIRL DETECTIVE HERE. WHEN LAWYER-DAD CARSON DREW ASKED ME ALONG TO ISTANBUL, TURKEY, HOW COULD I SAY NO?
HE WAS HERE TO OVERSEE THE SALE OF AN ANCESTRAL ESTATE BELONGING TO A CLIENT, ALDA OKTAR. MEANWHILE, THE THREE OF US TOOK IN THE SIGHTS, LIKE THIS PLACE, THE GRAND BAZAAR.
THE KAPALI CARSI, OR COVERED MARKET, HAS MILES OF PASSAGEWAYS AND OVER 4000 SHOPS! YOU'D THINK I'D HAVE LOTS TO LOOK AT, BUT I COULDN'T HELP BUT BE FASCINATED BY THE WAY MY DAD WAS STARING AT ALDA.
I THINK HE LIKED HER.
CHAPTER ONE: THE QUITE BIZARRE BAZAAR

THIS WAS *BIG* NEWS IN THE DREW FAMILY. MOM DIED WHEN I WAS THREE, AND I WAS ALWAYS WORRIED ABOUT DAD BEING LONELY. NOT TODAY, THOUGH.

I WAS FEELING A LITTLE LIKE A THIRD WHEEL, SO I STARTED LOOKING AROUND FOR AN EXCUSE TO... YOU KNOW... LEAVE THEM *ALONE* AWHILE.

BUT THE FIRST THING I SPOTTED WAS THIS HUGE *UGLY* STATUE.
I TRY HARD TO APPRECIATE OTHER CULTURES, AND I KNOW BEAUTY'S IN THE EYE OF THE BEHOLDER, BUT THIS THING WAS JUST... JUST...

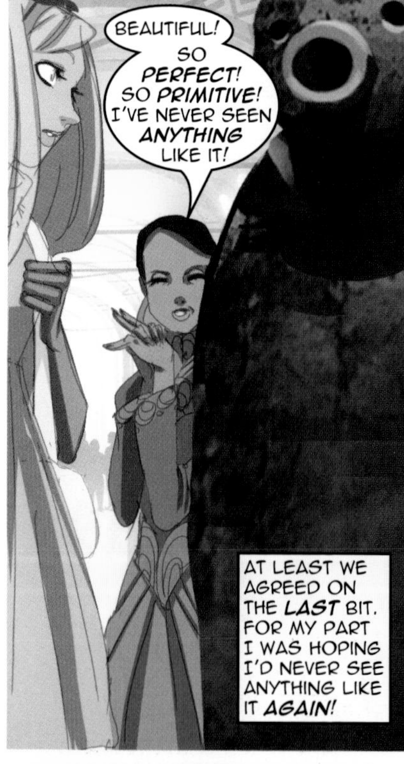

BEAUTIFUL! SO *PERFECT*! SO *PRIMITIVE*! I'VE NEVER SEEN *ANYTHING* LIKE IT!
AT LEAST WE AGREED ON THE *LAST* BIT. FOR MY PART I WAS HOPING I'D NEVER SEE ANYTHING LIKE IT *AGAIN*!

NOT SO MUCH WITH THE LUCK ON THAT ONE. SEEING HOW HAPPY IT MADE ALDA, MY GALLANT FATHER STEPPED UP AND STARTED BIDDING.
I KNOW WE'RE SUPPOSED TO HAGGLE, BUT I'VE NEVER BEEN VERY GOOD AT THAT.
WOULD YOU TAKE 200 LIRA FOR THE STATUE?
SOLD!
EVEN DAD COULD TELL THE GUY WAS A LITTLE TOO EAGER.
AHEM. SORRY, I MEANT 100.
STILL SOLD!
50?
NOT A KURUŞ MORE!
AND OF COURSE THAT INCLUDES SHIPPING TO MS. OKTAR'S HOME, YES?
INDEED! I'LL GIFT WRAP IT AND THROW IN A FREE CLOCK AS WELL!

YOU'RE **AWFULLY** AGREEABLE FOR A SALES-MAN!

SO? I LIKE TO MAKE PEOPLE **HAPPY**!

THEN MAKE **ME** HAPPY AND TELL ME WHY YOU WANT TO GET RID OF THE STATUE SO **BADLY**? DOES IT DISSOLVE IN WATER OR SOME-THING?
NO! IT'S NOT THAT THERE'S ANYTHING WRONG WITH IT! IT'S JUST A LITTLE...
...HAUNTED.

I IMAGINED MY PAL GEORGE SAYING, "BY WHAT, BAD TASTE?"

REALLY?

GOOD THING I DIDN'T BELIEVE IN GHOSTS. I DECIDED **NOT** TO MENTION IT TO ALDA OR MY DAD. WHY SPOIL **HER** ENJOYMENT OF THIS.... THIS... THING?

I'M SO GRATEFUL TO YOU FOR RENTING THIS LIMO, CARSON.

MY PLEASURE, ALDA.

BUT, I APOLOGIZE FOR NOT GETTING A ***LARGER*** CAR. AM I CRUSHING YOU?

I'M FINE. BUT ***YOU*** LOOK CRAMPED. PUT YOUR ARM AROUND ME IF IT WILL BE MORE COMFORTABLE!

JUST AS I WAS WISHING I WAS ONE OF THOSE DAUGHTERS WHO WEARS AN IPOD CRANKED UP LOUD...

...WE ARRIVED AT ALDA'S HOME.

TURKEY WAS ONCE PART OF THE ROMAN EMPIRE AND *THAT* ARCHITECTURE IS CALLED ***BYZANTINE***. THEN, IN THE 13TH CENTURY, CONQUERING TURKS STARTED BUILDING OTTOMAN ARCHITECTURE, SOME OF IT FIT FOR A SULTAN.
BEAUTIFUL, ISN'T IT? IT HAS BEEN IN MY FAMILY FOR CENTURIES.
BUT, THEN WHY ARE YOU ***SELLING*** IT?

ALDA'S ESTATE WAS A VERY COOL *COMBINATION* OF THE TWO STYLES. IT WAS LIKE SOMETHING OUT OF A FAIRY TALE.

I'VE HAD A RUN OF MONEY TROUBLES.

AND NOW... ⇉SIGH⇇, THINGS HAVE GOTTEN... WORSE.
HOW SO?

I RECENTLY HAD TO HAVE ONE OF MY SERVANTS ARRESTED FOR STEALING A PLAQUE THAT HAD BEEN WITH THE HOUSE SINCE THE OLDEST PART WAS FIRST BUILT.
HE WAS CAUGHT WITH IT IN HIS HANDS, BUT HE STILL WON'T CONFESS!

WE'LL GET THIS ALL SORTED OUT, I PROMISE.

YOUR MONEY TROUBLES WILL BE OVER SOON. ***HARLAND SEVERINO*** HAS MADE A VERY ***GENEROUS*** BID.

OF COURSE! ***HE'S*** BEEN DYING TO BUY IT FOR YEARS.

I REALIZE WE CAN'T ***REALLY*** PUT A PRICE ON YOUR ANCESTRAL HOME.

THIS MUST BE VERY PAINFUL.

MY DAD WAS PRETTY SENSITIVE TO ALDA'S SITUATION, BUT ***I*** WAS SENSING SHE MISSED THAT PLAQUE EVEN ***MORE*** THAN SHE WAS GOING TO MISS THE HOUSE.

BEFORE WE LEFT, I MADE SURE MY CELL PHONE COULD MAKE INTERNATIONAL CALLS SO I COULD ***CONNECT*** WITH MY BEST FRIENDS, BESS AND GEORGE.

THEY'RE COUSINS, BUT COULDN'T BE MORE DIFFERENT FROM EACH OTHER.

THEY'RE ALSO MY PARTNERS IN SLEUTHING. AND WHILE I DIDN'T HAVE ANY ***MYSTERIES*** TO REPORT, THEIR EARS PERKED UP ABOUT MY DAD'S LITTLE FLIRTATION WITH ALDA.

THEN I TOLD THEM ABOUT THE ALLEGEDLY HAUNTED, NOT SO ALLEGEDLY HIDEOUS STATUE...

...WHICH WAS BEING DELIVERED AS WE SPOKE. UNFORTUNATELY, THE ONLY MYSTERY SO FAR WAS HOW I WOULD STAND LIVING IN THE SAME HOUSE WITH IT.
OKAY. SO, TELL ALDA IT'S HAUNTED. SHE'LL FREAK OUT AND GET RID OF IT. PROBLEM SOLVED.

THANKS, GEORGE, BUT IT WOULDN'T BE POLITE.

I AGREE WITH GEORGE, NANCY! WHAT'S ***RUDE*** ABOUT IT?
YOU'D JUST BE PASSING ON INFORMATION THE STATUE'S OWNER ***SHOULD HAVE***.
THERE'S NOTHING TO WORRY ABOUT.

***YOU*** AGREE WITH ***ME***?
NOW, ***THAT'S*** SOMETHING TO WORRY ABOUT.

WISH YOU GUYS COULD **SEE** THIS PLACE. IT'S LIKE A ***MUSEUM***.

EVEN THE DOOR KNOB IS TOTALLY...

AHHHH!

TOTALLY AHHHH?! IS THAT TURKISH SLANG FOR FANCY?
NANCY?

NANCY?! WHAT'S WRONG?!

IT'S THE STATUE.

BUT WHAT'S IT DOING HERE?

OH, HELLO, NANCY. SORRY THEY BLOCKED YOUR DOOR. THE MAN IS HERE TO INSTALL IT.

OH, IT'S ALL RIGHT, THEN. IT'S JUST EN ROUTE TO...

...RIGHT *HERE*?!

I'VE BEEN LOOKING FOR SOMETHING TO COVER THAT UGLY *CRACK*. IT'S THE PERFECT THING, DON'T YOU THINK?

YOU'RE VERY SWEET, MY DEAR. BUT, I DON'T BELIEVE IN SUCH **NONSENSE**.

HEH. OF COURSE. I JUST THOUGHT YOU MIGHT FIND IT... **INTERESTING**.

I THOUGHT MAYBE IF I ***UNDERSTOOD*** THE STATUE, I'D APPRECIATE IT MORE, BUT I COULDN'T FIND ANYTHING ***LIKE*** IT IN ANY BOOKS.

FRANKLY, I WAS A LITTLE BORED. THE ONLY MYSTERY FOR ME TO THINK ABOUT WAS THAT THERE REALLY WAS NO ACCOUNTING FOR TASTE.

BUT IT HAD BEEN A ***LONG*** DAY, SO...

I WAS TOTALLY TENSE AND EXHAUSTED, BUT SLEEP ISN'T ALWAYS THE BEST WAY TO RELAX.
I DREAMED THE STATUE CAME TO LIFE...
...AND REDECORATED MY ROOM.

IT MOVED CLOSER AND CLOSER...
...MAKING A STRANGE KIND OF...
...POPPING SOUND.
POP!
POP!

POP!

I THOUGHT I WOKE UP...
POP!

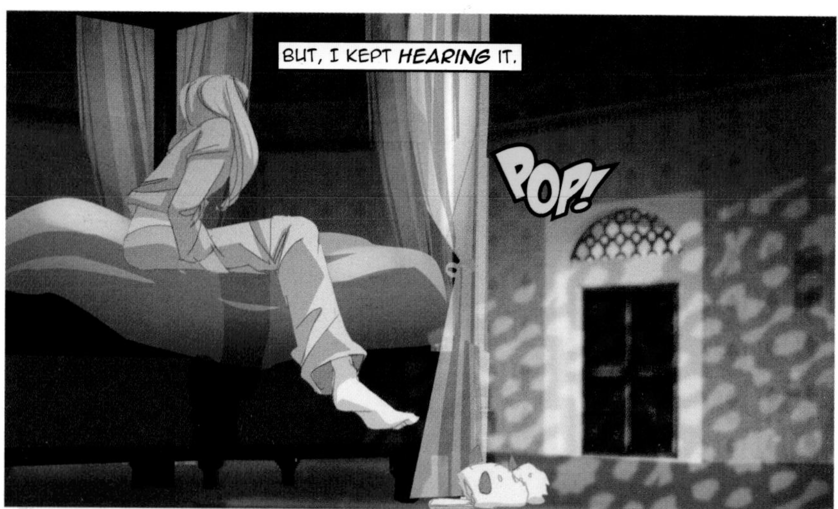
BUT, I KEPT HEARING IT.
POP!

I WAS DEFINITELY AWAKE... MY ROOM WAS, UH, TASTEFUL AGAIN.
BUT, THERE IT WAS STILL... EVERY FEW SECONDS...
...POP!
POP!

IT WAS COMING FROM THE HALL.
POP!

IT WAS CLOSE.
POP!

HMPH! NOTHING.

JUST *YOU*, MOCKING ME.

HUH.

I KNOW THAT THE POWER OF SUGGESTION IS PRETTY... WELL, ***POWERFUL***.

AND I DEFINITELY DON'T BELIEVE IN GHOSTS OR HAUNTED THINGS!

I PRIDE MYSELF ON BEING COMPLETELY LOGICAL...

...CONSIDERING ONLY THE ***FACTS*** IN ANY GIVEN SITUATION.

I KNOW THERE ARE ***SOME*** THINGS IN THIS WORLD THAT ***SEEM*** ***UN***EXPLAINABLE.

BUT, GENERALLY, THEY'RE ***NOT***!

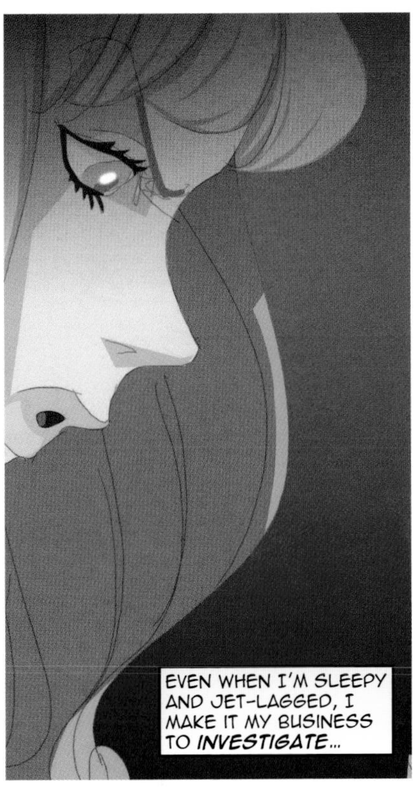

EVEN WHEN I'M SLEEPY AND JET-LAGGED, I MAKE IT MY BUSINESS TO *INVESTIGATE*...

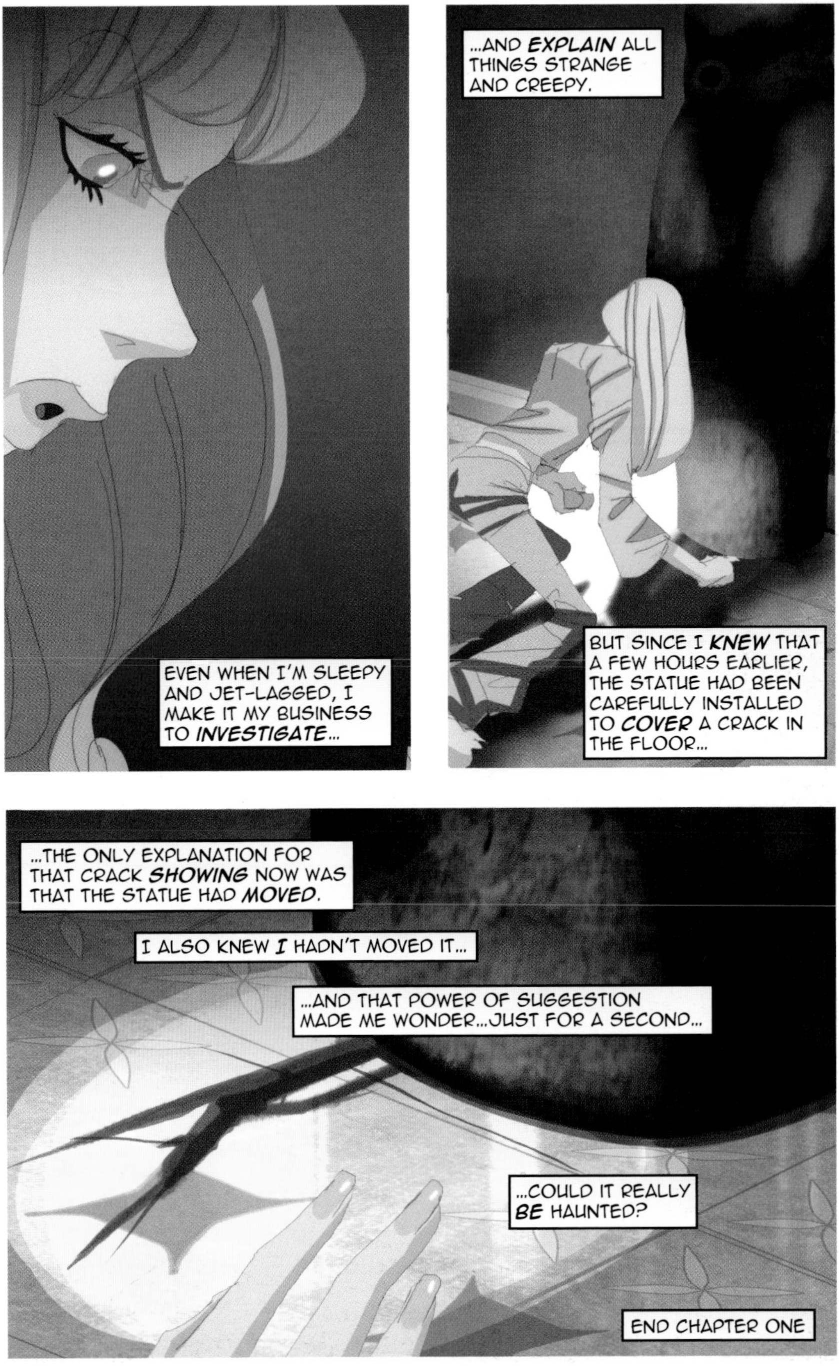

...AND *EXPLAIN* ALL THINGS STRANGE AND CREEPY.
BUT SINCE I *KNEW* THAT A FEW HOURS EARLIER, THE STATUE HAD BEEN CAREFULLY INSTALLED TO *COVER* A CRACK IN THE FLOOR...

...THE ONLY EXPLANATION FOR THAT CRACK *SHOWING* NOW WAS THAT THE STATUE HAD *MOVED*.

I ALSO KNEW *I* HADN'T MOVED IT...

...AND THAT POWER OF SUGGESTION MADE ME WONDER...JUST FOR A SECOND...

...COULD IT REALLY *BE* HAUNTED?

END CHAPTER ONE

SLEEPING THAT NIGHT WAS A LITTLE ***HARDER*** THAN I'D LIKE TO ADMIT.

BUT, BY EARLY MORNING I'D SHAKEN OFF MY PARANORMAL PARANOIA.

HAVVA, WHY WASN'T THIS PLATE CLEARED?

BUT MISTRESS, I ***CLEARED ALL*** THE DINNER DISHES LATE LAST NIGHT!

# CHAPTER TWO: STATUE OF IMITATION

APPARENTLY, THE HALLWAY OUT-SIDE MY BEDROOM WASN'T THE ONLY PART OF THE HOUSE WHERE THINGS WERE OUT OF PLACE.
THAT DISH WAS NOT THERE WHEN I WENT TO BED!

STRANGE. PERHAPS ONE OF OUR GUESTS HAD A LATE SNACK.
HMM. WASN'T ME. AND MY DAD HAD A BIG DINNER BEFORE GOING TO BED EARLY...
...SO HE WASN'T THE LIKELY MIDNIGHT SNACKER.

ALDA SEEMED STRESSED. I FIGURED IT WAS A BAD TIME TO MENTION MY STATUE'S SLIGHTLY ALTERED LOCATION.
SO I DECIDED TO WAIT AND KEEP AN EYE ON THINGS.

AFTER A LONG DAY OF ***SIGHT-SEEING*** EVERYONE WENT TO BED ***EARLY***. THE HOUSE WAS VERY QUIET...

UNTIL...

AHHHHHHH!

I HEARD A SCREAM! IT SOUNDED LIKE HAVVA! HER ROOM IS AROUND THE CORNER.
THE SECOND FLOOR WAS SHAPED LIKE A SQUARE WITH FOUR SEPARATE HALLWAYS.
I WAS ON ONE. DAD AND ALDA WERE ON ANOTHER.

THE SERVANTS' ROOMS, FOR HAVVA AND ALDA'S NOW ARRESTED MAN-SERVANT, WERE ON A THIRD HALLWAY.

I HEARD THIS ODD POPPING! I GOT UP TO CHECK AND... I... I SAW A SHADOW MOVING... THERE.

I DON'T SEE ANY-THING.
NEITHER DO I...
EXCEPT *THAT!*

NANCY?!

NOW I'VE GOT--

--YOU?!

I WAS EXPECTING SOMETHING MORE INTERESTING, BUT NOT NECESSARILY MORE ATTRACTIVE.
AM I CRAZY OR DID YOU MOVE AGAIN?

WHAT WAS IT?
I'M NOT SURE HOW ANY HUMAN BEING COULD'VE MADE IT ALL THE WAY DOWN THE HALL BEFORE I TURNED THE CORNER.

BUT, I GUESS THEY DID.

THAT MORNING, THE PLOT THICKENED. ALDA DISCOVERED SOME SMALL HEIRLOOMS WERE MISSING.

IT WAS TIME TO TELL SOMEONE ABOUT THE STATUE. GIVEN HOW UPSET ALDA WAS, I THOUGHT I'D BETTER START WITH MY DAD.

BUT, IT SEEMS HE HAD SOMETHING PRIVATE TO DISCUSS WITH ME!

TURNS OUT IT WAS THE SAME SOMETHING... SORT OF.

NANCY, I'M SORRY TO ASK THIS, BUT I KNOW YOU DON'T LIKE THAT STATUE AND I KNOW YOUR FRIENDS THOUGHT YOU SHOULD MAKE ALDA THINK IT WAS HAUNTED...

BUT, I ALSO KNOW YOU WOULDN'T... COULDN'T POSSIBLY INDULGE IN SUCH NONSENSE... WOULD YOU?!

DAD! HOW COULD YOU EVEN ASK? OF COURSE NOT!

SORRY. PLEASE... JUST PUT UP WITH THE THING, FOR ALDA'S SAKE, OKAY?
SURE, DAD.
EITHER DAD'S HEAD WAS SO TURNED BY ALDA IT WAS GETTING UNUSUALLY *MUDDLED*, OR SOMEONE ELSE HAD PUT THAT IDEA IN HIS HEAD.

ALL RIGHT, WHICH ONE OF YOU TOLD MY DAD THAT CRAZY IDEA ABOUT PRETENDING THE STATUE WAS HAUNTED?

NOT ME!

NOT ME!

BUT WE *MIGHT* HAVE BEEN TALKING ABOUT THAT WHEN YOUR DAD PICKED UP YOUR PHONE --
WHICH YOU *DROPPED*, NANCY!

METHINKS THE LACK OF SLEEP IS AFFECTING SOMEONE'S DETECTING, GIRL!
RIGHT. PERFECT!

THE PROBLEM IS, NOW DAD WON'T KNOW WHETHER TO BELIEVE ME OR NOT IF I *DO* TELL HIM THERE'S SOMETHING WEIRD ABOUT THAT UGLY STATUE!

OUR SIGHTSEEING THAT DAY WAS A LITTLE MORE ON THE SERIOUS SIDE. IT STARTED AT POLICE HEADQUARTERS, WHERE ALDA'S SERVANT, RASHIK, WAS BEING HELD.
DAD HAD FINALLY ARRANGED FOR THE RELEASE OF THE PLAQUE RASHIK HAD BEEN CAUGHT WITH.
ALDA, MEANWHILE, HAD ASKED TO MEET WITH THE FORMERLY FAITHFUL RASHIK. HIS FAMILY HAD SERVED HER FAMILY FOR AS FAR BACK AS ANYONE COULD REMEMBER, AND SHE NEEDED TO UNDERSTAND WHAT HAPPENED.
WHILE DAD FILLED OUT THE PAPERWORK, ALDA ASKED ME TO SIT IN ON HER VISIT WITH RASHIK.
I WAS SURPRISED TO HEAR SHE STILL HADN'T PRESSED CHARGES AND SEEMED CONFUSED ABOUT WHAT TO DO.

ALDA HOPED TO GET A CLUE FROM RASHIK. BUT EVEN NOW, THE STRANGELY ***EXPRESSIONLESS*** MAN HAD SAID ***NOTHING*** IN HIS OWN DEFENSE.

RASHIK, I JUST DON'T UNDERSTAND... HOW ***COULD*** YOU..?

PLEASE JUST ***TELL*** ME ***WHY*** YOU STOLE THE PLAQUE?!

AFFECTION FOR SOMEONE YOU'VE LIVED WITH ALL YOUR LIFE IS ONLY NATURAL...

...BUT YOU DIDN'T HAVE TO BE A DETECTIVE TO SENSE SOMETHING MORE... SOME ***DEEPER*** EMOTION BETWEEN THEM.

NANCY, I WONDER IF YOU COULD GIVE ME A MOMENT ALONE WITH RASHIK?

DON'T WORRY. I'LL BE FINE.

I WASN'T WORRIED ABOUT LEAVING HER ALONE WITH HIM. MAYBE IT WAS JUST CURIOSITY THAT MADE ME HESITATE.

WHILE ALDA TRIED TO SOLVE HER MYSTERY, I SET OFF TO GET SOME ***ANSWERS*** OF MY OWN.

STARTING WITH FINDING THE ***OLD MAN*** WHO SOLD MY DAD THE STATUE IN THE FIRST PLACE.

BUT, ***NO ONE*** SEEMED TO KNOW THE LITTLE MAN WITH THE BEARD AND THE UGLY STATUE.

AFTER WALKING AROUND FOR AN HOUR OR MORE, I FOUND MYSELF STANDING AT WHAT I WAS SURE WAS THE ***EXACT SPOT*** WHERE WE'D BOUGHT THE STATUE.

ONLY, EVERYTHING WAS GONE.

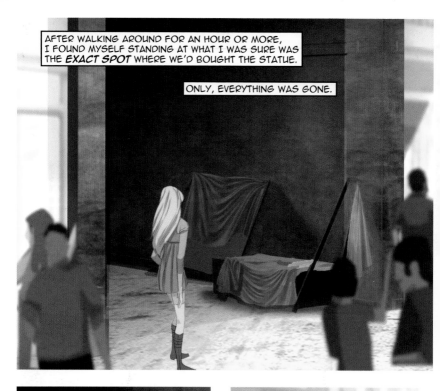

NOT EVERYTHING. APPARENTLY THE OLD MAN LEFT IN A HURRY -- LIKE A CARTOON CHARACTER, HE'D RACED OFF LEAVING HIS BEARD BEHIND.

BUT NOT BEFORE HE'D BLOWN A MONSTER BUBBLE. THE BEARD WAS COVERED WITH CHEWING GUM.

SOMEHOW, I IMAGINED AN OLD STREET VENDOR BEING MORE INTO CHEWING TOBACCO THAN GUM.

WELL, AT LEAST **SOMETHING** IS BACK TO NORMAL!
I'D HOPED SHE'D SMILE, BUT IT WAS PRETTY CLEAR ALDA WAS STILL FEELING ANYTHING **BUT** NORMAL, AND FINDING LITTLE COMFORT IN THAT COLD BRASS PLAQUE.

I JUST DON'T KNOW WHAT I WOULD DO WITHOUT YOU AND NANCY HERE, CARSON.

I'M JUST **SO** GRATEFUL!

THAT NIGHT I KEPT WONDERING, WHAT ***WOULD*** ALDA DO IF WE WEREN'T HERE? SHE SEEMED SO SAD IT COULDN'T JUST BE THE HOUSE, NOT EVEN A HOUSE AS GREAT AS ***THIS***.

IT FELT LIKE ANOTHER PIECE IN A ***BIG*** PUZZLE.

OH, WELL. THE DARK QUIET CAN BE A GREAT TIME FOR CONNECTING PUZZLE PIECES IN YOUR HEAD.

ALDA'S SADNESS... THE BEARD... RASHIK... THE PLAQUE... THE STATUE... ALL FIT TOGETHER TO MAKE A STORY, BUT I COULDN'T QUITE GET --

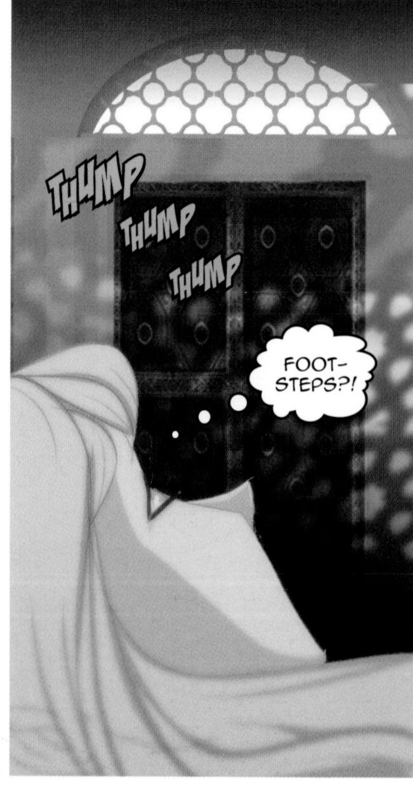

THUMP
THUMP
THUMP
FOOT-STEPS?!

YEP. DEFINITELY FOOTSTEPS.

THUMP

THUMP

THUMP

MUCH AS I WOULD HAVE LIKED IT TO, I WAS STILL *PRETTY* SURE THE STATUE DIDN'T JUST GET UP AND WALK AWAY.

THUMP
THUMP
THUMP

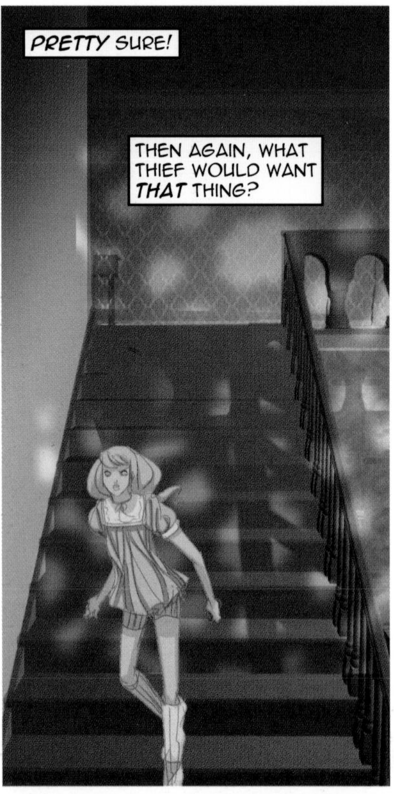

*PRETTY* SURE!
THEN AGAIN, WHAT THIEF WOULD WANT *THAT* THING?

GREAT. THESE STEPS GO TO THE BASEMENT. NO LIGHTS.

IF I TURNED MY FLASH-LIGHT ON, WHOEVER I WAS FOLLOWING MIGHT SEE IT.
BUT *I* COULDN'T SEE ***ANYTHING*** WITHOUT IT.

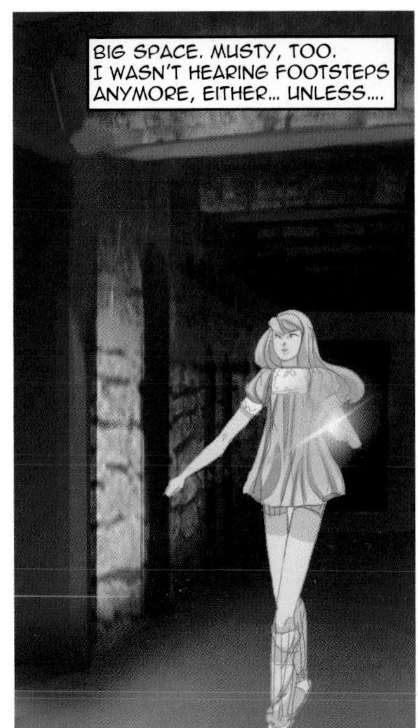
BIG SPACE. MUSTY, TOO. I WASN'T HEARING FOOTSTEPS ANYMORE, EITHER... UNLESS....

*HMPH!* HOW MANY ***BASEMENTS*** CAN THERE BE IN THIS PLACE?!

I WISH I HADN'T ASKED!
TURNED OUT THERE WERE *PLENTY!*
ONE EMPTY BASEMENT LED TO ANOTHER...
AND *ANOTHER*...

AND EACH BASEMENT SEEMED *OLDER* THAN THE LAST.
I STARTED TO FEEL LIKE I WAS...
...GOING BACKWARDS...

...THROUGH *TIME*.

IF THIS WAS ***ANOTHER*** WEIRD DREAM, I WAS STARTING TO MISS THE FIRST ONE WITH THE UGLY STATUE AND THE LOUSY DÉCOR!

FINALLY, I SAW **ANOTHER** LIGHT AND HEARD SOME SCRAPING SOUNDS.

AND FRANKLY, I WASN'T FEELING TOO **GOOD** ABOUT IT. I MEAN, HECK, I WAS ALL **ALONE** DOWN HERE.

CHK!

CHK!

SCRAPE!

FORGET GETTING A CELL PHONE SIGNAL, NO ONE WOULD HEAR ME **SCREAM** IF SOMETHING HAPPENED. NO ONE WOULD EVER **FIND** ME!

OH, WELL. NO ONE EVER SAID BEING A DETECTIVE WAS EASY. I TURNED OFF MY FLASHLIGHT AND MOVED FORWARD, BEING AS QUIET AS I COULD.
CHK!
CHK!
SCRAPE!

SO, I COULD SEE BUT NOT BE SEEN. ODDS ARE WHATEVER IT WAS WOULDN'T HEAR ME WITH THAT RACKET IT WAS MAKING.
CHK!
CHK!
SCRAPE!
IF I MANAGED NOT TO GASP TOO LOUDLY THAT IS!

AGAIN, NOT EXACTLY WHAT I WAS EXPECTING. INSTEAD OF GETTING A WHOLE PICTURE, I WAS ONLY GETTING MORE PUZZLE PIECES!
WHO WERE THESE GUYS? THEY CERTAINLY DIDN'T LOOK LIKE *PLUMBERS!* WHAT WERE THEY DIGGING FOR? AND WHY DID THEY HAVE *ALDA'S PLAQUE*???

I WASN'T PLANNING TO ASK THEM. AT LEAST NOT UNTIL AFTER I GOT HELP!

I STARTED BACKING AWAY, AS SLOWLY AND CAREFULLY AS I COULD.

NOT SO CAREFUL, I GUESS. AFTER A FEW FEET, I HIT SOMETHING. COULD IT BE A WALL ALREADY?

NOPE. HAUNTED STATUE.
END CHAPTER TWO

CHAPTER THREE:
LOOK OUT BELOW
GASP

THE THIEVES' OBVIOUS LEADER WASN'T GLAD TO SEE ME.

BASA KIZ!

I HADN'T LEARNED MUCH TURKISH, YET...

DURMA, EY KÜÇÜK PICKTON!

...BUT I WAS TRANSLATING THE BODY LANGUAGE WHICH SEEMED PRETTY ***CLEAR***...

...THAT IF I LIKED LIVING, I SHOULD RUN!
AND ***KEEP*** RUNNING!

UNK!
UNGH!
CLACK

MY FLASHLIGHT WAS NO MATCH FOR A PICK AXE...

NO!

FINALLY, WE HAVE YOU!
ONE OF THE MEN SPOKE ENGLISH. HE SOUNDED AMERICAN. STILL, I DIDN'T UNDERSTAND...

...WHAT DID HE MEAN BY 'FINALLY'?
IT WAS YOU ALL ALONG! WASN'T IT? CONFESS!

HEY, YOU DEFINITELY AREN'T WEARING THE LATEST IN HELPFUL CITIZEN ATTIRE AND FRANKLY, I'M NOT BIG ON CONFESSING TO CROOKS!

I'M NOT EVEN SURE WHAT YOU'RE ACCUSING **ME** OF, BUT IF THERE'S ANYTHING **YOU'D** LIKE TO GET OFF **YOUR** CHESTS...

DON'T PRETEND! YOU'VE BEEN TRYING TO SPOOK US WITH THAT **MOVING STATUE**!
HAH! I TOLD YOU IT WAS A **FAKE**!
**STATUE?**

*I* WAS THINKING IT WAS *YOU* GUYS.
KIND OF *HOPING*, ACTUALLY.
HUH?

WHAT ARE YOU *LOOKING* AT?

IF IT WASN'T ***THEM*** FAKING THE MOVING STATUE, AND IT CERTAINLY WASN'T ***ME***...

COULD IT ***REALLY*** BE HAUNTED?

OYNAYAN TERK!-- YOU PUT IT THERE!

NO! I JUST RAN AND TRIPPED HERE! YOU SAW ME!

WAIT. SHE'S RIGHT-- WE RAN PAST THE STATUE... BACK THERE BEFORE WE CAUGHT HER!

WHAT'S THAT?!
POP!

POP!

POP!
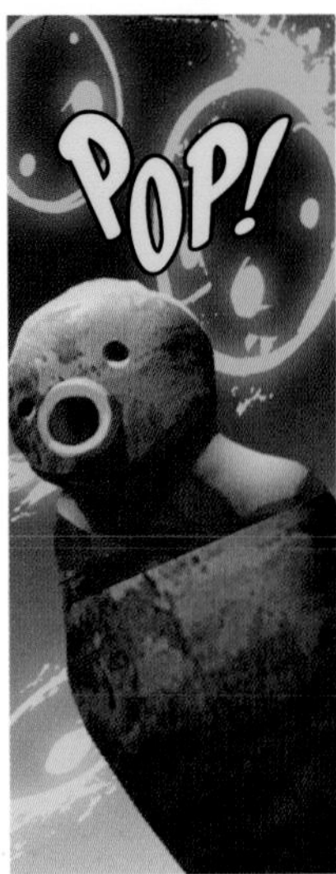
POP!

POP!

MOAN

SHFF
SHFF
SHFF
IT... IT'S **ALIVE!**
WHAT DO WE DO?!!
DON'T PANIC! THIS **CAN'T** BE WHAT IT LOOKS LIKE...

WHY DON'T YOU GO INVESTIGATE, THEN?
HEY!
I HAVE TO ADMIT, NOT PANICKING WAS EASIER SAID THAN DONE!
SHFF
SHFF
SHFF

I DIDN'T ***LIKE*** THIS THING FROM THE START...

...AND MY REASONS FOR HATING IT WERE ONLY INCREASING...
SNIFF WHAT'S THAT SMELL?

BUT, THEN I NOTICED SOMETHING ABOUT IT...
...SOMETHING KIND OF... SWEET!
BUBBLE GUM?

PANT
THE GIRL, THE, THE STATUE, IT'S...
I'VE DONE IT! I'VE UNCOVERED THE LOCK!

NOW TO PLACE THE KEY!
KACHAK

GGRRGGGCCCHHHH

GOOD LORD!

SHFFF
SHFF
FORGET THE GIRL AND THE STATUE! LET'S GO!

WHATEVER THEY FOUND WAS PRETTY IMPORTANT...
...OR MAYBE *I* JUST WASN'T IMPORTANT!
WHATEVER THE REASON, THEY LEFT *ME* AT THE MERCY OF THE HAUNTED STATUE!

BUT, FORTUNATELY, SOMEONE ELSE *DID* CARE WHAT HAPPENED TO ME.
NANCY! ARE YOU OKAY?!

YOU WEREN'T IN YOUR **BED**, THE BASEMENT DOORS WERE **OPEN**, WE KEPT SEARCHING DEEPER AND **DEEPER**...
WHAT ARE YOU DOING DOWN **HERE**?!

SOLVING MYSTERIES! WELL, ONE OUT OF **TWO**, ANYWAY!

THE STATUE?! BUT, HOW...?
KNOCK KNOCK
HEY! COME OUT OF THERE, PLEASE!

DAD'S CONCERN FOR MY *SANITY* ENDED QUICKLY AS THE STATUE *OPENED* UP.

BUT, THE LITTLE 'GHOST' INSIDE GAVE US *ALL* A NEW CONCERN.

COMPARED TO OUR OTHER PROBLEMS, THIS WAS A *RELIEF*!

STAND BACK! HE'S GONNA BLOW!

YOU'D THINK I'D BE USED TO THESE TENSE MOMENTS...

BUT THIS WAS A LITTLE OUT OF MY LEAGUE.
POP!
OH!

HELLO!

WHO ARE YOU?! YOU THINK IT'S FUN TO SCARE THE ***WITS*** OUT OF PEOPLE?!

WAIT! CARSON, I KNOW HIM!

THAT EXPLAINS THE POPPING NOISES AND THE GUM IN THE BEARD I FOUND.

I'LL EXPLAIN...
NO, LET ME GUESS! IT'S WHAT I DO!

YOU WANTED TO GET INTO THE HOUSE TO TRY AND PROVE YOUR FATHER'S INNOCENCE, RIGHT?
YES!

WELL, THAT... AND I LIKE HAVVA'S FOOD BETTER THAN MY AUNT'S.

I'M SO SORRY, TOVIK! I KNOW YOU LOVE YOUR FATHER, BUT, IF RASHIK WERE INNOCENT, WHY WOULD HE REMAIN SILENT?

MY DAD IS INNOCENT! HE WAS PROTECTING THE PLAQUE, BECAUSE HE KNEW THOSE MEN WANTED TO STEAL IT!
AND TONIGHT, THEY DID!

WHAT?!
WHAT MEN,
TOVIK?

THREE OF THEM. ONE TALL, ALL WEARING SKI-MASKS... DESPITE THE DISTINCT LACK OF SNOW.

THEY WERE LOOKING FOR SOMETHING HERE.

THE SECRET OF THAT PLAQUE MUST BE PRETTY ***IMPORTANT*** FOR RASHIK TO GO TO JAIL RATHER THAN TALK ABOUT IT.

IT LOOKS LIKE IT ACTED AS SOME SORT OF ***KEY***!

NOW, I KNEW WHY THE BUYER WAS SO EAGER TO GET ALDA'S HOUSE!
THE PLACE HAD THE BIGGEST FINISHED BASEMENT I'VE EVER SEEN!!
TO BE CONTINUED...

PECIAL PREVIEW OF NANCY DREW GRAPHIC NOVEL #18 – "CITY UNDER THE BASEMENT"

NANCY DREW, GIRL DETECTIVE, HERE TO TELL YOU THAT NO MATTER WHERE YOU GO, DARK IS STILL DARK.
AND NOT ONLY AM I CLIMBING DOWN A DEEP DARK HOLE, I'M TOTALLY IN THE DARK ABOUT A MAJOR MYSTERY.
SEE, I CAME TO TURKEY WITH MY DAD, CARSON, SO HE COULD HELP SELL ALDA OKTAR'S ANCESTRAL ESTATE.

SHE WAS UPSET WHEN RASHIK, A TRUSTED SERVANT, WAS CAUGHT STEALING A PLAQUE. TO CHEER HER UP, DAD BOUGHT HER THIS UGLY, SUPPOSEDLY HAUNTED STATUE.
IT DID GET AROUND, EVEN TO THE MANY SUB-BASEMENTS, WHERE I FOLLOWED AND LEARNED RASHIK'S SON TOVIK WAS HIDING INSIDE, HOPING TO CLEAR HIS DAD'S NAME.
HE'D FOLLOWED THREE THIEVES WHO'D TAKEN THAT PLAQUE AND USED IT TO OPEN A DOOR TO AN ENTIRE ANCIENT CITY BENEATH THE HOUSE!

WHY IS THERE A CITY UNDER THE BASEMENT? WHAT DO THOSE THIEVES WANT? THAT'S WHAT I PLAN TO FIND OUT.
IF I SURVIVE!
SEE WHAT I MEAN ABOUT THE DARK?

CHAPTER ONE:
SECRETS OF THE HIDDEN CITY
NICE, CATCH, DAD!
URK! THANKS, BUT I THINK I TWISTED MY SHOULDER!
CARSON, ARE YOU ALL RIGHT?

I DIDN'T MIND THAT ***ALDA*** WAS MORE WORRIED ABOUT DAD THAN ME. IT WAS PRETTY OBVIOUS HE LIKED HER, AND I WAS HOPING SHE FELT THE SAME.

WE SHOULDN'T HAVE COME DOWN HERE!

SHE'S RIGHT, NANCY, EVEN IF IT ***IS*** AMAZING!

BUT WE COULDN'T RISK LETTING THOSE CROOKS GET AWAY, AND TOVIK WILL HAVE THE POLICE HERE IN ***NO*** TIME!

BETTER HOPE YOU'RE ***WRONG*** ABOUT THAT!

***DON'T MISS NANCY DREW GRAPHIC NOVEL #18 – "CITY UNDER THE BASEMENT"***

# THE HARDY BOYS

## A NEW GRAPHIC NOVEL EVERY 3 MONTHS!

#12 "Dude Ranch O' Death"
ISBN - 978-1-59707-088-1
#13 "The Deadliest Stunt"
ISBN - 978-1-59707-102-4
#14 "Haley Danielle's Top Eight!"
ISBN – 978-159707-113-0
#15 "Live Free, Die Hardy!"
ISBN – 978-159707-123-9
NEW! #16 "SHHHHHH!"
ISBN – 978-159707-138-3
Also available – Hardy Boys #1-11
All: Pocket sized, 96-112 pp., full-color, $7.95
Also available in hardcover! $12.95

THE HARDY BOYS
Graphic Novels #1-4 Box Set
ISBN – 978-1-59707-040-9
THE HARDY BOYS
Graphic Novels #5-8 Box Set
ISBN – 978-1-59707-075-1
THE HARDY BOYS
Graphic Novels #9-12 Box Set
ISBN-978-1-59707-125-3
All: Full-color, $29.95

**CLASSICS** *Illustrated*
Featuring Stories by the World's Greatest Authors

#1 "Great Expectations"
ISBN 978-159707-097-3
#2 "The Invisible Man"
ISBN 978-159707-106-2
#3 "Through the Looking-Glass"
ISBN 978-159707-115-4
NEW! #4 "The Raven and Other Poems"
ISBN 978-159707-140-6
All: 6 1/2 x 9, 56 pp., full-color, $9.95



Please add $4.00 postage and handling. Add $1.00 for each additional item.
Make check payable to NBM publishing. Send To:
Papercutz, 40 Exchange Place, Suite 1308,
New York, New York 10005, 1-800-886-1223

www.papercutz.com

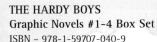

NANCY DREW girl detective®
AND
THE HARDY BOYS
NOW READ THEIR ADVENTURES ON YOUR MOBILE PHONE!
ON THE WEB:
WWW.GOCOMICS.COM/COMICBOOKS
ON YOUR MOBILE PHONE:
M.GOCOMICS.COM
gocomics™
PAPERCUTZ

# WATCH OUT FOR PAPERCUTZ

Welcome to the backpages of NANCY DREW Graphic Novel #17 "Night of the Living Chatchke." In case you're still wondering, a "chatchke," (or chatchka or tchotchke) is a knick-knack, or an inexpensive souvenir, or worthless piece of junk. See how educational a Papercutz graphic novel can be?

Around the same time we're sending NANCY DREW #17 to our printers (Happy Year of the Ox, printers!) we're also going back to press for the big eighth printing of the Girl Detective's comics debut --- NANCY DREW #1 "The Demon of River Heights." In fact, that graphic novel, along with THE HARDY BOYS graphic novel #1 "The Ocean of Osyria," published in early 2005 were the debut graphic novels from a little company called Papercutz (that's us!).

Since that historic premiere printing ND #1 has gone through all sorts of changes and minor tweaks. Perhaps the biggest was a few printings ago, when NANCY DREW artist Sho Murase decided to make some incredible changes to the color art. If you compare the latest printings to the first, you'll see that many pages have been virtually recolored, looking even more vibrant and dramatic than before. And here's the amazing part – Sho decided to make all these changes on her own. We were completely pleased with the earlier color work, but Sho the perfectionist wasn't, and she took it upon herself to give this graphic novel a gorgeous upgrade.

We're so happy to have Sho onboard as NANCY DREW's regular artist – she's done every cover, and every graphic novel except #5 and #7 – as she's captured that special essence that has made Nancy Drew America's favorite Girl Detective. Of course, we mustn't forget Stefan Petrucha, who has written every graphic novel based on Carolyn Keene's super-sleuth. Stefan's writer-wife Sarah Kinney has recently joined Stefan in creating scripts, and the stories and mysteries are getting even more exciting than ever before.

Papercutz publisher Terry Nantier and I (Jim Salicrup, editor-in-chief) are proud to report that thanks to our readers' loyal support, Papercutz is not only still producing four all-new NANCY DREW and four all-new HARDY BOYS graphic novels every year, but we're also publishing quite a few other titles you may love just as much as NANCY DREW. On the next few pages we talk a lot about CLASSICS ILLUSTRATED and CLASSICS ILLUSTRATED DELUXE, which we're sure you'll enjoy.

Now there's just enough room left to thank you! Yes, YOU! We greatly appreciate you're picking up this graphic novel, and hope you enjoyed it as much as we enjoyed putting it together. Let us know what you think, send your comments to me at salicrup@papercutz.com or by mail to Jim Salicrup, PAPERCUTZ, 40 Exchange Place, Ste 1308, New York, NY 10005. And be sure to check us out at www.papercutz.com for all the latest new developments!

Thanks,
Jim

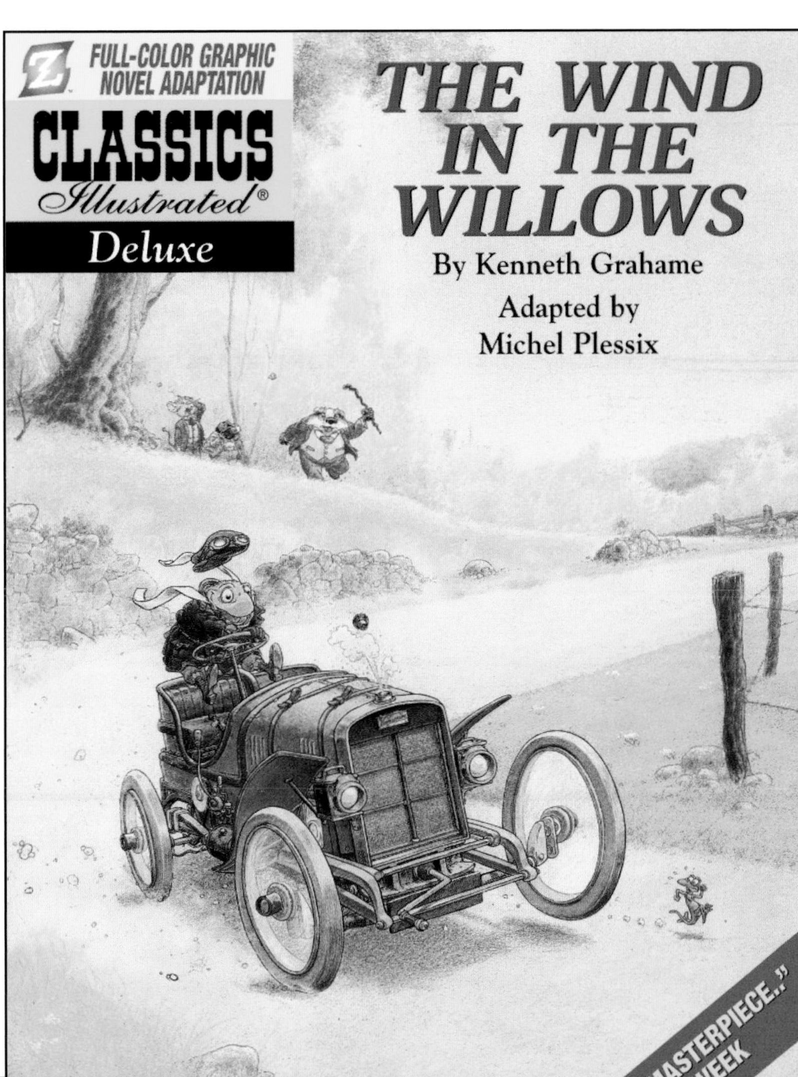
FULL-COLOR GRAPHIC NOVEL ADAPTATION
CLASSICS Illustrated®
Deluxe
THE WIND IN THE WILLOWS
By Kenneth Grahame
Adapted by
Michel Plessix
PAPERCUTZ
"A VISUAL MASTERPIECE."
-NEWSWEEK

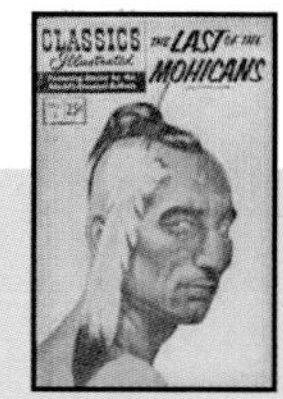

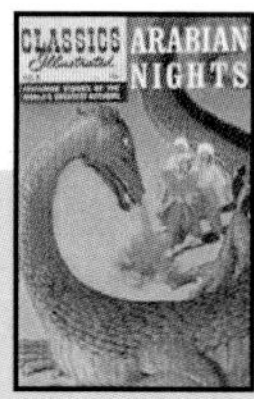

# A Short History of CLASSICS ILLUSTRATED...

*William B. Jones Jr. is the author of Classics Illustrated: A Cultural History, which offers a comprehensive overview of the original comic-book series and the writers, artists, editors, and publishers behind-the-scenes. With Mr. Jones Jr.'s kind permission, here's a very short overview of the history of CLASSICS ILLUSTRATED adapted from his 2005 essay on Albert Kanter.*

CLASSICS ILLUSTRATED was the creation of Albert Lewis Kanter, a visionary publisher, who from 1941 to 1971, introduced young readers worldwide to the realms of literature, history, folklore, mythology, and science in over 200 titles in such comicbook series as CLASSICS ILLUSTRATED and CLASSICS ILLUSTRATED JUNIOR. Kanter, inspired by the success of the first comicbooks published in the early 30s and late 40s, believed he

could use the same medium to introduce young readers to the world of great literature. CLASSIC COMICS (later changed to CLASSICS ILLUSTRATED in 1947) was launched in 1941, and soon the comicbook adaptations of Shakespeare, Stevenson, Twain, Verne, and other authors, were being used in schools and endorsed by educators.

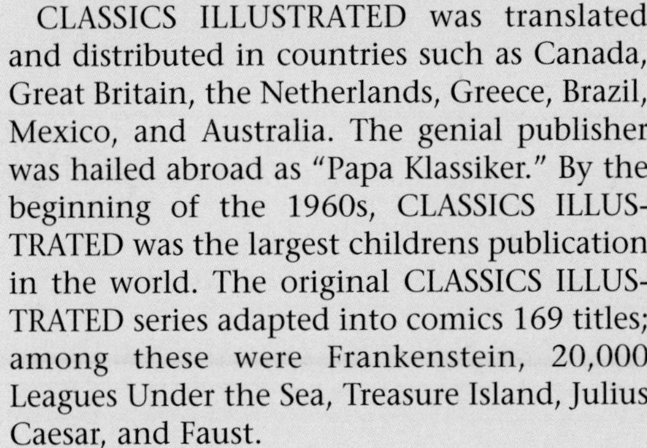

CLASSICS ILLUSTRATED was translated and distributed in countries such as Canada, Great Britain, the Netherlands, Greece, Brazil, Mexico, and Australia. The genial publisher was hailed abroad as "Papa Klassiker." By the beginning of the 1960s, CLASSICS ILLUSTRATED was the largest childrens publication in the world. The original CLASSICS ILLUSTRATED series adapted into comics 169 titles; among these were Frankenstein, 20,000 Leagues Under the Sea, Treasure Island, Julius Caesar, and Faust.

Albert L. Kanter died, March 17, 1973, leaving behind a rich legacy for the millions of readers whose imaginations were awakened by CLASSICS ILLUSTRATED.

CLASSICS ILLUSTRATED was re-launched in 1990 in graphic novel/book form by the Berkley Publishing Group and First Publishing, Inc. featuring all-new adaptations by such top graphic novelists as Rick Geary, Bill Sienkiewicz, Kyle Baker, Gahan Wilson, and others. "First had the right idea, they just came out about 15 years too soon. Now bookstores are ready for graphic novels such as these," Jim explains. Many of these excellent adaptations have been acquired by Papercutz and will make up the new series of CLASSICS ILLUSTRATED titles.

The first volume of the new CLASSICS ILLUSTRATED series presents graphic novelist Rick Geary's adaptation of "Great Expectations" by Charles Dickens. The second volume, is also by Geary, featuring his adaptation of "The Invisble Man" by H. G. Wells. The third volume, an adaptation of "Through the Looking-Glass" the follow-up to "Alice's Adventures in Wonderland" by Lewis Carroll, is by Harvey and Eisner award-winning graphic novelist Kyle Baker. The fifth features "The Raven and Other Poems" by Edgar Allan Poe and illustrated by *The New Yorker* and *Playboy* cartoonist Gahan Wilson – a sample of which appears on the following pages.

## ALONE

From childhood's hour I have not been
As others were— I have not seen
As others saw— I could not bring
My passions from a common spring.
From the same source I have not taken
My sorrow; I could not awaken
My heart to joy at the same tone;
And all I lov'd, *I* lov'd alone.

*Then*— in my childhood— in the dawn
Of a most stormy life— was drawn
From ev'ry depth of good and ill
The mystery which binds me still:
From the torrent, or the fountain,
From the red cliff of the mountain,
From the sun that 'round me roll'd
In its autumn tint of gold—
From the lightning in the sky
As it pass'd me flying by—
From the thunder and the storm,
And the cloud that took the form
(When the rest of Heaven was blue)
Of a demon in my view.